To Charles Perrault and the Brothers Grimm, and to all the authors of fairy tales.
What we inherited from them is an extraordinary source of inspiration.
O. D.

For my dad, Marcellin.
G. D.

First American Edition 2020
Kane Miller, A Division of EDC Publishing

Dessine-moi une histoire
Published in Belgium in 2019 by Éditions Mijade
© 2019 Mijade Publications (B-5000 Namur - Belgium)
Geneviève Després for the illustrations
Olivier Dupin for the text
English text adapted from a translation by Jane Singleton Paul

For information contact:
Kane Miller, A Division of EDC Publishing
P.O. Box 470663
Tulsa, OK 74147-0663
www.kanemiller.com
www.edcpub.com
www.usbornebooksandmore.com

Library of Congress Control Number: 2019947446

Printed in Belgium

2 3 4 5 6 7 8 9 10
ISBN: 978-1-68464-047-8

Olivier Dupin   Geneviève Després

Draw Me A Story

Kane Miller
A DIVISION OF EDC PUBLISHING

When Anna was little, she loved stories.
All kinds of stories.

But fairy tales were her favorite.

Once upon a time there was a little girl named Little Red Riding Hood …

Suddenly, a voice cried out, "Yoo-hoo! Hello? I've just about had it!"

Anna looked around.
"Right here!" the voice said.

Little Red Riding Hood was staring right at her.
"Yes, yes, it's me. I've had it up to here.
Every time you read this story, I end up in the wolf's belly."

Anna thought for a moment.
Maybe ...

She grabbed her felt-tip pens, and …

"Thank you," said Little Red Riding Hood.
"That's much better!"

The next night, Anna had just opened her book when …

"No! Not again!" said Tom Thumb.

"I'm tired of being abandoned in the forest.
And I don't want to go to that house with the ogre.
I just want to go for a bike ride."

Anna got her pens again, and Tom Thumb and his brothers
went on a long bike ride through the forest.
They were thrilled.
And they told everyone about it.

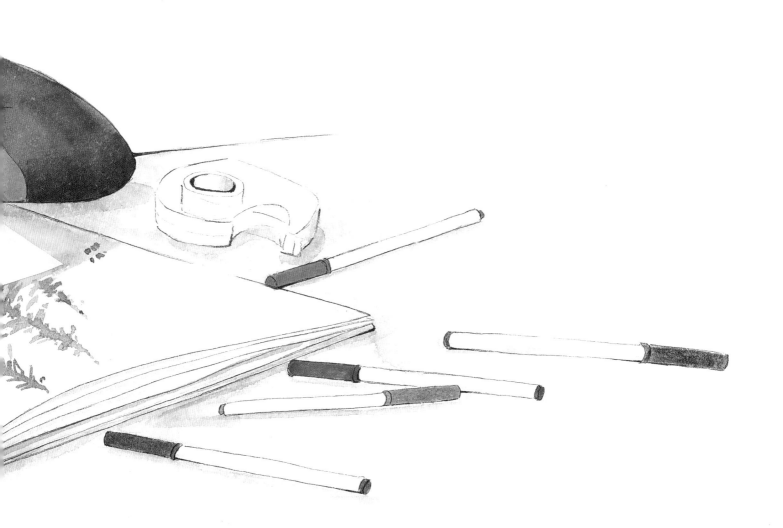

Suddenly, all their friends wanted new adventures too.

The Three Little Pigs wanted to save their houses.
Goldilocks was sick of porridge.
Cinderella just wanted a bath …

Anna took out a brand-new notebook – she felt bad about drawing in her books – and got to work.

It took a long, long time, but finally …
"Ready?" she called.

Little Red Riding Hood played hide-and-seek
with the Three Little Pigs.
Tom Thumb went bowling.
Cinderella and Goldilocks went horseback riding.

They had a wonderful lunch, and everyone was very happy.

Well, not quite everyone.

"What about us?"
The Big Bad Wolf, the Three Bears,
the Wicked Witch … they all wanted new adventures too.
So Anna wrote and drew, and wrote and drew…

And she never stopped!
(And that's how Anna became an illustrator.)